THE HOITY-TOITY ANGEL

Caroline Hoile

Illustrated by Hazel Quintanilla

spck

There was once a very beautiful angel.
Her hair gleamed, her wings sparkled and
her dress was whiter than white.

She was the most elegant angel that you could ever have wished to see.

But she was also very, very proud.

She really thought that she was the best!

Now one day God sent another angel, Gabriel, to a little town called Nazareth to give a young girl called Mary a most important message.

The Angel Gabriel appeared in front of Mary and said...

'You are going to have a very special baby and you must call him Jesus.'

Mary was absolutely amazed to hear this news!

All the other angels were very excited by this news, too, but not the Hoity-Toity Angel.

She thought Mary looked far too ordinary.
She wasn't even a princess!

So she glared at the other angels and began
to create a terrible fuss.

'I am the greatest!' she proudly proclaimed.
'Only the *very* best is good enough for me! I can't
possibly be seen with that ordinary-looking young girl!
And I won't ever sing to her!'

At this the stars twinkled nervously
and the other angels shook their heads at her.

'Don't be so hoity-toity!' they exclaimed.
'Looks don't matter one little bit.
It's what you're like inside that counts!'

The Hoity-Toity Angel frowned.
She knew that if she didn't join in, she wouldn't be allowed
to sing to the new baby king when he was born ...
and she badly wanted to do that!

So she stamped her foot crossly.

'Bother!' she said. And she pulled a terrible face.
But she snootily agreed to sing.

One cold, dark night, some shepherds were out on the hillside looking after their sheep.

Suddenly a fantastic angel appeared in front of them.

The shepherds were absolutely terrified. They had never seen an angel before!

But the angel told them not to worry.

'Tonight a very special baby has been born in Bethlehem,' the angel said. 'You must go and visit him!'

The shepherds were very excited by this news.
The baby king had been born!

But the Hoity-Toity Angel looked at the shepherds
with alarm. They looked so scruffy!

She glared at the other angels and
began to create a terrible fuss.

'I am the greatest!' she proudly proclaimed.
'Only the *very* best is good enough for me!
I can't possibly be seen with those scruffy
shepherds! And I won't sing to them, either!'

At this, the stars twinkled nervously
and the other angels shook their heads at her.

'Don't be so hoity-toity!' they exclaimed.
'Looks don't matter one little bit.
It's what you're like inside that counts!'

The Hoity-Toity Angel frowned.
She knew that if she didn't join in, she wouldn't be
allowed to sing to the new baby king...
and she badly wanted to do that!

So she stamped her foot crossly.

'Bother!' she said. And she pulled a terrible face.
But she snootily agreed to sing.

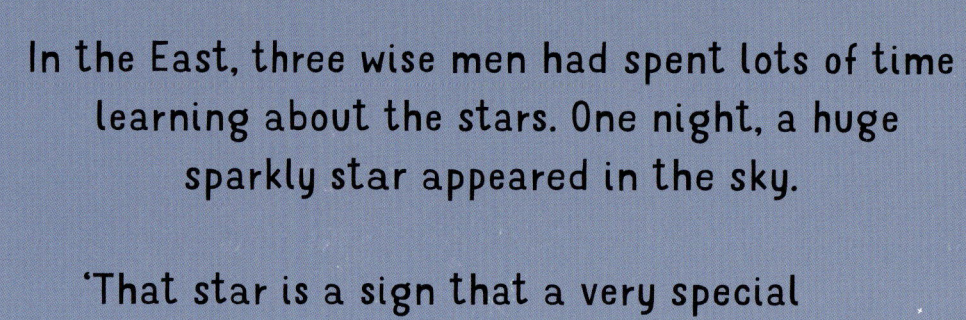

In the East, three wise men had spent lots of time learning about the stars. One night, a huge sparkly star appeared in the sky.

'That star is a sign that a very special baby has been born,' they said. 'We *must* follow it!'

And off they went.

After a long time, the three wise men arrived at King Herod's palace in Jerusalem. They politely asked him where they would find the special baby.

'In Bethlehem!' King Herod replied. Then he added sneakily 'I'd like to visit him too.'

But Herod actually didn't want to see the baby at all. He just wanted to get rid of him!

The Hoity-Toity Angel looked at the three wise men with approval. They looked so handsome! She watched as they visited King Herod in his palace.

'A palace!' she shrieked. 'With a proper king inside!'

And she began to make a terrible fuss!

'I am the greatest!' she proudly proclaimed. 'Only the very best is good enough for me! *Do* let me sing to those *wonderful* three wise men and that *very* rich king in his palace. It's *just* my sort of place and they're *quite* the sort of people I need to be seen with!'

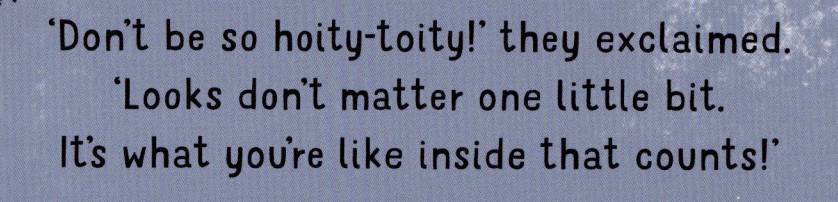

At this, the stars twinkled nervously
and the other angels shook their heads.

'Don't be so hoity-toity!' they exclaimed.
'Looks don't matter one little bit.
It's what you're like inside that counts!'

Then they added quite seriously,
'You can't possibly sing there.
That is not where we are supposed to sing at all.'

The Hoity-Toity Angel frowned and stamped her foot crossly.

'Bother!' she said. And she pulled a terrible face.
But she didn't sing one note!

Meanwhile, in Bethlehem, a very special baby had indeed been born. His name was Jesus.

Mary and Joseph wrapped the little baby in some soft cloth to keep him warm and placed him in the manger filled with straw.

The shepherds arrived at the stable
with their sheep and their little lambs.
They went inside and knelt down quietly.
They gave the baby their woolly lambs as a gift.

The three wise men followed the spectacular star all the way to the stable in Bethlehem.

They knelt down on the dusty floor and gave baby Jesus their precious gifts of gold, frankincense and myrrh.

The angels appeared at the stable too.

'This is where the baby king has been born,' they exclaimed. 'We're *so* pleased to be here!'

'But where is the baby king?' asked the Hoity-Toity Angel proudly. 'This old place just can't be right! And that surely can't be him lying in the manger with straw poking out all around him?!'

The Hoity-Toity Angel glared at the other angels and began to create a terrible fuss.

'I am the greatest!' she proudly proclaimed.
'Only the *very* best is good enough for me!
I can't possibly be seen singing to a baby king lying in a manger in this old broken-down stable. I just can't!'

And she pulled a terrible face!

The other angels were horrified!
They shook their heads at the Hoity-Toity Angel.

'This baby is the best, the very, very best!' they said.

And they swiftly pushed her into the stable!

The Hoity-Toity Angel tripped over on to the dirty stable floor.

'Ugh!' she said with disgust.

She picked herself up, and what a sight she was!

Her wings were crooked.

Her hair was in a mess.

Her face was filthy...

...and her dress was torn.

She looked absolutely dreadful!

The Hoity-Toity Angel looked across nervously at the baby king. Whatever was he going to think of her now?

Then, all at once, as she gazed at the tiny baby,
the Hoity-Toity Angel saw how proud she had always been,
and how badly she had behaved. And she felt so very sorry!

Baby Jesus looked at the sorry, scruffy angel
and he smiled at her with joy.

And instantly, the Hoity-Toity Angel glowed with happiness!

'Now I understand!' she exclaimed.
'Looks don't matter one little bit, do they?
It's what you're like inside that counts. And now that
I've met the baby king, I feel like a brand
new angel inside!'

The other angels
cheered with delight.

The Hoity-Toity Angel smiled a happy smile.
And she was never hoity-toity again!

For Lucy, Emily and Sam. My three hoity-toity angels . . .

First published in Great Britain in 2019

Society for Promoting Christian Knowledge
36 Causton Street, London SW1P 4ST
www.spck.org.uk

Text copyright © Caroline Hoile 2019
Illustrations copyright © Hazel Quintanilla 2019

All rights reserved. No part of this book may be reproduced or transmitted in any form or by any means, electronic or mechanical, including photocopying, recording, or by any information storage and retrieval system, without permission in writing from the publisher.

British Library Cataloguing-in-Publication Data
A catalogue record for this book is available from the British Library

ISBN 978–0–281–07784–7

Typeset by Sue Mason
Printed by Imago

Produced on paper from sustainable forests